FRANK
AND BEAN

FRANK
AND BEAN

JAMIE MICHALAK
illustrated by BOB KOLAR

CANDLEWICK PRESS

To Frank and Mary
J. M.

For Ruby and Julia
B. K.

First paperback edition 2022

Library of Congress Catalog Card Number 2019939114
ISBN 978-0-7636-9559-0 (hardcover)
ISBN 978-1-5362-2197-8 (paperback)

21 22 23 24 25 26 CCP 10 9 8 7 6 5 4 3 2 1

Printed in Shenzhen, Guangdong, China

This book was typeset in New Century Schoolbook.
The illustrations were created digitally.

Candlewick Press
99 Dover Street
Somerville, Massachusetts 02144

www.candlewick.com

CONTENTS

Chapter 1

FRANK

This is Frank.

This is Frank's tent.

This is Frank's pencil.

This is Frank's spork.

This is Frank's secret notebook.

Everything here is Frank's.

"Alone at last!" says Frank. "Now I can write in peace."

Frank writes in his notebook.

But then he hears *ribbit, ribbit.*

"Sorry, frog," he says. "My writing is top secret."

Frank moves on.

Frank hikes.

He writes in his notebook.

Hoo, hoo.

"Shoo, you!" he says. "No peeking at my words, owl."

Frank moves again.

Frank dips his toes in the pond.

He writes in his notebook.

Splish! Splash!

"Good gravy!" he shouts. "Who is it now? You can't read my secret notebook. And that's that!"

He looks down.

"Oh! It's just me," he says. "Silly Frank."

At night Frank toasts one lonely marshmallow.

"Good night, frog!" he says. "Good
night, owl! Good night, crickets!"
The frog does not say good night.
The owl does not say good night.

The crickets do not say good night.
None of them say good night to Frank.
Frank frowns.
"Good night, Frank," says Frank.

Chapter 2
BEAN

Frank eats his oatmeal.

He writes in his secret notebook.

But then he hears . . .

HONK, HONK, HONK!

"Good gravy!" cries Frank. "What is THAT?"

Something parks next to Frank's tent.

This is Bean.

This is Bean's bus.

This is Bean's trumpet.

This is Bean's drum.

This is Bean's triangle . . . and motorbike . . . and gong.

Everything here is Bean's.

Bean plays his trumpet.

TOOT, TOOT!

Frank frowns. "That is too loud."

Bean plays his drum.

BOOM, BOOM!

"Oh, no," says Frank. "That is even louder."

Bean tries to sing. ***"I AM A BEAN WITHOUT A SONG. DOO-DEE-DOO . . . BOO-HOO!"***

"Enough is enough!" says Frank. "Stop making so much noise!"

Bean gives up trying to sing.

He rides his motorbike.

VROOM, VROOM!

"You are loud," says Frank.

"NO, I'M NOT!" Bean shouts.

"I AM BEAN!"

"I am Frank," says Frank. "What are you doing here?"

"YOU WANT ME TO CHEER?" yells Bean. "OK. HOORAY FOR FRANK!"

"I did not say cheer," says Frank. "Turn off your bike so I can talk with you."

"MOO?" Bean shouts. "DO I HEAR A COW?"

"I said YOU," says Frank. "Not MOO!"

Bean looks around. "THERE IS THAT COW AGAIN," he says.

Frank says, "I give up. Goodbye."

"GOOD PIE?" calls Bean. "I WOULD LOVE SOME. THANKS!"

Bean follows Frank back to his tent.

Chapter 3

LOUD AND MESSY

"Where is the pie?" asks Bean.

"Pie? What pie?" Frank asks.

"Oh, rats! Did you give it to the cow?" asks Bean.

Frank sighs. "Are you lost?"

"No. I am on a journey," says Bean. "I am looking for something. I have searched from sea to sea."

"What are you looking for?" Frank asks.

"Words," says Bean.

"*Words?* Why?" asks Frank.

"Because I am a one-bean band," says Bean. "I make up tunes. But I have no words to sing with them. I have tried and tried. But I cannot write a song."

"You are trying too hard," says Frank. "You don't need to look far for words."

"I don't?" asks Bean.

"No. The words are already inside you. But you are too loud to hear them," says Frank. "Try this: Sit still. Then be quiet."

Frank is as still as a rock.
All is quiet.

SQUIRT!

"Bean! That is not quiet," says Frank.

"Being quiet makes me hungry," says Bean. "Want a jelly doughnut hole?"

"No. I've never had one. Now *shh*," says Frank. He closes his eyes.

All is quiet again.

SQUIRT! SPLAT!

"You are loud *and* messy," says Frank.

"What is on your hat?" Bean asks.

"That is my headlamp," says Frank.

"Give it back."

"What is this?" Bean asks. "Three . . . two . . . one . . . FIRE!"

"That is my spork," says Frank. "It is half fork and half spoon."

"Wow! A spork is half cool and half amazing," says Bean.

"What is this?" asks Bean.

"DO NOT TOUCH!" Frank yells.

"Why?" asks Bean.

"That's my secret notebook," says Frank.

"Why is it secret?" asks Bean. "Are you a spy? Are you a robber? Do you steal sporks?"

"No," says Frank.

"I know what you are," says Bean. "You are a private eye."

"No! Will you *ever* be quiet?" says Frank.

"Yes. When you try a jelly doughnut hole," says Bean. "TRY IT."

"Fine," says Frank. "But just one small bite."

CHOMP!

SQUIRT!

SPLAT!

MMM.

GULP.

BURP.

"Hot diggity dog," Frank says.

"That is more than one small bite," says Bean.

Frank does not say a word. He writes in his secret notebook.

Chapter 4

THE BIG SECRET

Frank closes his secret notebook.

He turns off his headlamp.

He shuts his eyes.

All is quiet.

TOOTY-TOOT, TOOT!

"Good gravy!" says Frank.

He knocks on Bean's door. *Tap, tap, tap.*
"Have you come to hear my trumpet?"
asks Bean.

"No! It is too late for tooting,"
says Frank. "Be quiet."
Frank goes back to bed.
All is quiet again.

Tap, tap, tap!

"Bean! Do you know what time it is?"
Frank asks.

"Yes," says Bean. "It is time to rock."

"NO," says Frank. "It is time to sleep."

Frank goes back to bed.

All is . . .

"HELLO, FRANK. IT IS I, BEAN!"

"Bean!" says Frank. "What are you doing here?"

"Being a one-bean band is lonely," says Bean. "Nobody knows when I am scared. I hear monsters. Listen!"

Ribbit, ribbit.

"Those are not monsters," says Frank. "Those are frogs."

Hoo, hoo.

"Yikes! What is that?" Bean asks.

"Those are owls," says Frank.

Chirr, chirr.

"AND WHAT ARE THOSE SCARY
MONSTERS?" Bean asks.

"Those are crickets," says Frank. "Do
not be afraid. Listen again."

Bean sits as still as a rock.

Ribbit, ribbit. Hoo, hoo. Chirr, chirr.

"It sounds like music," says Bean.

"It is," says Frank. "It is the night's song."

Bean hums. *Ribbit, ribbit. Hoo, hoo. Chirr, chirr.*

"I have a new tune!" says Bean. "All I need now are words."

"Hmm," says Frank. He opens his secret notebook.

"What is so secret anyway?" Bean asks.

Frank frowns. "I want to tell you. But what if you laugh at me?"

"Do not worry," says Bean. "I am not a mean bean."

"OK. I will tell you," says Frank. "These are my poems. But sharing them is scary."

"Please read a poem," says Bean. "Do not be afraid."

"I will try," says Frank. "I will be brave."

Bean hums the night's tune.

Frank sings his new poem:

"You are small, loud, and messy.
But inside you are sweet.
Oh, jelly doughnut hole!
You are fun to eat."

"That is my new favorite song," says Bean.

Frank and Bean sing the Jelly Doughnut Hole Song together.

"You did it, Frank!" says Bean. "You wrote a song. Now I know what you are. You are not a spy or a private eye."

"Then what am I?" asks Frank.

"You are a rock star," says Bean. "Want to be in my band?"

"In a word," says Frank, "yes."

"Cool beans!" says Bean. "I can be quiet now, Frank. I will go to bed."

"Good night, frog," says Frank. "Good night, owl. Good night, crickets."

The frog does not say good night.

The owl does not say good night.

The crickets do not say good night.

None of them say good night to Frank.

"Good night, Bean," Frank whispers.

"SWEET DREAMS, FRANK!" yells

Bean.